To
Gregory and Marc
Marissa and Alexandre
to celebrate their early years

—W. J. S.

To
my daughters
Stephanie and Alison
in whom the sun rises and sets

—C.R.

Sing a song of seasons!
    Something bright in all!
Flowers in the summer,
    Fires in the Fall!

— Robert Louis Stevenson

NEW YEAR'S DAY

New Year's Day

The sun is up, the sky is clear:
A bright new day, a bright new year.

—William Jay Smith

JANUARY

White Fields

In the winter time we go
Walking in the fields of snow;

Where there is no grass at all;
Where the top of every wall,

Every fence and every tree,
Is as white as white can be.

Pointing out the way we came,
Every one of them the same—

All across the fields there be
Prints in silver filigree;

And our mothers always know,
By our footprints in the snow,

Where it is the children go.

—James Stephens

FEBRUARY

February Twilight

I stood beside a hill
Smooth with new-laid snow,
A single star looked out
From the cold evening glow.

There was no other creature
That saw what I could see—
I stood and watched the evening star
As long as it watched me.

—Sara Teasdale

My Valentine

I will make you brooches and toys for your delight
Of bird-song at morning and star-shine at night.
I will make a palace fit for you and me
Of green days in forests and blue days at sea.

—Robert Louis Stevenson

MARCH

March

A blue day,
a blue jay
and a good beginning.

One crow,
melting snow—
spring's winning!

—Elizabeth Coatsworth

Kite Days

A kite, a sky, and a good firm breeze,
And acres of ground away from trees,
And one hundred yards of clean, strong string—
O boy, O boy! I call that Spring!

—Mark Sawyer

APRIL

April

April has come, and all the hills
Are banked with violets and bluebells.
Buds break open, small birds sing
A song of welcome . . . It is spring!

—William Jay Smith

First Day of April

On the first day of April
if someone should say,
"I'll give you a monster,
a basket of hay,
a ride in a rocket,
and ten games to play,"
just laugh and remember . . .
It's APRIL FOOL'S DAY!

—Vivian Gouled

MAY

Maypole Dance

Swing round with the season,
Dance out in the sun;
Come circle the Maypole
For May has begun.
Weave rainbows of ribbon
Above the green lawn;
Bring baskets of flowers
As fresh as the dawn.
Swing round with the season,
Dance out in the sun;
Come circle the Maypole
For May has begun.

—Carol Ra

Maytime Magic

A little seed
For me to sow . . .

A little earth
To make it grow . . .
A little hole,
A little pat . . .
A little wish,
And that is that.

A little sun,
A little shower . . .
A little while,
And then—a flower!

—Mabel Watts

JUNE

A Day in June

In a soft blue sky white clouds appear,
The days grow longer—summer's here.
We lie in the shade by bubbling streams
And build cloud castles in our dreams.

—William Jay Smith

Kick a Little Stone

Kick a little stone and it
Hops ahead of you—
The little stone is round and white
Its shadow round and blue—
Along the pavements, over the cracks,
The shadow bounces too:
A very friendly little sight
A cheerful thing to do.

—Dorothy Aldis

JULY

In July

Tomatoes turn from green to red,
Flowers fill the flower bed
In July.

Up through grass and tangled briar
Fireflies flash as they climb higher
In July.

Rockets zoom through thick dark air
And sparks spray down like golden hair;
Flags unfurl and bugles blare
In celebration everywhere
In July.

—Carol Ra

At the Seaside

When I was down beside the sea
A wooden spade they gave to me
To dig the sandy shore.

My holes were empty like a cup
In every hole the sea came up,
Till it could come no more.

—Robert Louis Stevenson

AUGUST

August Afternoon

Where shall we go?
What shall we play?
What shall we do
On a hot summer day?

We'll sit in the swing.
Go low. Go high.
And drink lemonade
Till the glass is dry.

One straw for you,
One straw for me,
In the cool green shade
Of the walnut tree.

—Marion Edey

SEPTEMBER

September

A time of magic to remember,
A time of harvest and work done;
Gold is the color of September,
And purple, like the setting sun.

—William Jay Smith

OCTOBER

October

The month is amber,
Gold, and brown.
Blue ghosts of smoke
Float through the town.

Great V's of geese
Honk overhead,
And maples turn
A fiery red.

Frost bites the lawn.
The stars are slits
In a black cat's eye
Before she spits.

At last, small witches,
Goblins, hags,
And pirates armed
With paper bags,

Their costumes hinged
On safety pins,
Go haunt a night
Of pumpkin grins.

—John Updike

NOVEMBER

Down! Down!

Down, Down!
Yellow and brown
The leaves are falling over the town.

—Eleanor Farjeon

First Thanksgiving

Venison for stew and roasting,
oysters in the ashes toasting,
geese done to a turn,
berries (dried) and wild grapes (seeded)
mixed with dough and gently kneaded—
what a feast to earn!

Indian corn in strange disguises,
ash cakes, hoe cakes (many sizes),
kernels roasted brown . . .
after months of frugal living
what a welcome first Thanksgiving
there in Plymouth town!

—Aileen Fisher

DECEMBER

First Snow

Snow makes whiteness where it falls.
The bushes look like popcorn-balls.
And places where I always play,
Look like somewhere else today.

—Marie Louise Allen

Winter Moon

How thin and sharp is the moon tonight!
How thin and sharp and ghostly white
Is the slim curved crook of the moon tonight!

—Langston Hughes

CHRISTMAS

Christmas Tree

They brought the tree in from the snowbound wood
And through its branches did bright garlands weave
Until with lights and tinkling bells it stood
To welcome all of us on Christmas Eve.

—William Jay Smith

Christmas in the Olden Time

Heap on more wood! The wind is chill;
But let it whistle as it will,
We'll keep our Christmas merry still.

—Sir Walter Scott

NEW YEAR'S EVE

New Year's Eve

The stars are out, the sky is clear;
The bells ring in a bright new year.

Happy New Year!

Happy New Year!

—William Jay Smith

HAPPY NEW YEAR!